THE
LITTLE
PICKPOCKET

THE
LITTLE
PICKPOCKET

AVNER KATZ

Simon & Schuster Books for Young Readers

SIMON & SCHUSTER BOOKS FOR YOUNG READERS
An imprint of Simon & Schuster Children's Publishing Division
1230 Avenue of the Americas, New York, New York 10020
Copyright © 1996 by Avner Katz
All rights reserved including the right of reproduction
in whole or in part in any form.
SIMON & SCHUSTER BOOKS FOR YOUNG READERS
is a trademark of Simon & Schuster.
Book design by Paul Zakris
The text of this book is set in 18-point Garamond Semibold
The illustrations are rendered in acrylic
Manufactured in the United States of America
First Edition
10 9 8 7 6 5 4 3 2 1

Library of Congress Cataloging-in-Publication Data

Katz, Avner.
[Kayas ha-katan. English]
The little pickpocket / Avner Katz.
p.   cm.
Summary: Because his mother's pocket is too noisy,
Joey hops out to find a better one and has an interesting
adventure as he explores various pockets.
[1. Kangaroos—Fiction.   2. Pockets—Fiction.]   I. Title.
PZ7.K1567Li   1996   [E]—dc20   95-33394   CIP   AC

ISBN: 0-689-80494-6

To Yotam
—A. K.

Little Joey tossed and turned inside his mother's pouch, but it was no use. He just couldn't fall asleep. His parents were making too much of a racket outside.

"How is a kangaroo supposed to get any rest around here?" he muttered to himself. "There has got to be a better place to take a nap."

Joey climbed out of the pouch. His parents were so busy talking that they didn't even notice him leave.

Joey hopped off to find a better pocket.

Soon he spied a fancy lady with a pocket hanging
from her arm. "It doesn't look like my mother's,"
he thought, "but I'll give it a try."

He jumped in and tried to make himself
comfortable, but there were too many lumps
in the way. "This pouch smells
funny, too," he thought
with a sneeze.

Joey hopped out again. "Definitely not me," he said.

Before long he came upon a pocket belonging to
a rascally little boy. Joey peered inside. "Hmm,
maybe this one will suit me."

But no sooner had he climbed in than he sprang right back out again. "Yikes!" he said. "Too much wildlife in there. I wonder if they are looking for a new pouch, too."

Little Joey hopped on. When he saw a roomy, soft-looking pocket, he dove right in.

And fell right out. "Who ever heard of a pouch with a hole in the bottom?" the kangaroo complained as he rubbed his bruised head.

Unfazed, Joey tried out the next pocket he came across. "This one could be interesting," he told himself.

"Colorful," he thought, "but not my style."

Next Joey tried settling into a schoolboy's knapsack.

He learned a few things, but the book on *How to Sleep in a Strange Pouch* was missing.

By this time Joey was growing hungry. Fortunately, the next pouch he found belonged to a girl with a good appetite. Her pocket was full of tasty treats.

Soon the pocket was empty, but Joey was too full. "I think I'm going to be sick," he said.

Luck was with him again. The next pouch he tried
belonged to a doctor.

"Ah, I feel better now,"
Joey said to himself.
"But I need a pocket
that isn't so busy all
the time."

The next pouch was a big improvement. He liked the sounds he heard there.

Soon he was singing along with the music. Then it dawned on him: This was the lullaby his mother always sang to him.

When the song was over, Joey felt a little sad. He climbed out of the musician's pocket and thought for a moment.

Suddenly he sprang up. He jumped down the hillside, hurdled fences, leaped across streams, and hopped over bushes and trees.

Little Joey took one last big leap, straight into his mother's arms. Gently she tucked Joey into her pocket, the best pocket in the whole wide world.